D0281892

PROMISES

ILMFG
by Kathryn White

Published by Ransom Publishing Ltd.
Unit 7, Brocklands Farm, West Meon, Hampshire GU32 1JN, UK
www.ransom.co.uk

ISBN   978 178591 259 7
First published in 2016

Copyright © 2016 Ransom Publishing Ltd.
Text copyright © 2016 Kathryn White
Cover photograph copyright © apomares. Photograph page 4 copyright © zegers06
A CIP catalogue record of this book is available from the British Library.

All rights reserved. No part of this publication may be reproduced, stored in a
retrieval system, or transmitted, in any form or by any means, electronic, mechanical,
photocopying, recording or otherwise, without the prior permission of the publishers.

The right of Kathryn White to be identified as the author of this Work has been
asserted by her in accordance with sections 77 and 78 of the Copyright, Design and
Patents Act 1988.

ILMFG

(I LOVE MY FRIEND'S GUY)

Kathryn White

Ransom

one

Bad news!

I love my best friend's guy.

It's not *just* that Luke is fit. He's a cool guy too – and great fun.

But I love **MBF**, Roz, soooo much. She's like my twin. Maybe that's why we *like* the same guy.

I need help. I need to talk to someone so that I can sort this mess. But, no one must know who I am.

So, I've hit on this probs page. I can log on with a new ID and get info. But I'm kind of a wimp.

If I do this – what will happen?

It's 11p.m. and I'm in my jim–jams.

I'm sitting in bed with my fingernail on the keyboard.

I think, 'Hmm, I will do this.'

'I will not.'

'I will.'

'I will not.'

OMG! I did it.

Tap tap.

It's on the net.

> **Y-me?:**
>
> I'm Y-me? HELP! ILMFG.

It's OK.

No stress!

No one will know that **Y-me?** is really me, Abi Blue.

So, I'll stay cool and forget about it, for sure.

I'll just go to sleep.

♥

It's 1 a.m.

I'm still in my jim-jams.

This is not fun.

I can't sleep.

I turn this way. I turn that way.

I stick my legs in the air.

I blow my hair off my nose with a '*fuff*'.

I rub my eyes.

I pull my curls until – yow!

I make silly noises. 'Hom, hee, ho, hom, hee ho.'

I count, one sheep, two sheep, what have I done sheep?

I still can't sleep.

ILU – Luke.

TWO

Monday morning. I'm chilled.

Yeah right!

As long as no one knows that
I posted **ILMFG** on the web, then I will

keep **MBF** Roz. If Roz knew, she'd never talk to me again.

No, *worse*! She'd hate me.

I don't hate Roz, even if she is going out with **2D4** Luke.

It's not fair, but no way do I hate Roz.

Well – not *all* of the time.

Only when Luke is holding her hand, or they're snogging.

Arghghghgh!

I do not hate, Roz.

No time for brekker, so I grab a smoothie on my way to school and hope no one knows **Y-me?** is me.

♥

It's 9.15 a.m.

I'm late into school.

I plod in the door like my feet are made of clay.

I'm pooped.

I was up all night.

The **ILMFG** on line was buzz, buzzing in my head like a mad bee.

If I had put **ILMFG** on paper, I would have tossed it in the bin by now.

But, that's the thing about the net.

When you send stuff out, it gets hooked in like a big, fat, smelly fish.

I keep looking around to see if anyone knows that I'm **Y-me?**.

I'm jumpy.

Mum says I think too much – so I try not to think and just smile.

I smile at the gross kid who is making faces at me.

I smile at our head, Mr Tod, who is a grump. Mr Tod tuts at me for being late. Grump!

I smile just to chill out.

It's **MUFTY**. Today we can wear what we want.

I'm in red. Luke loves red, he told me last week.

Stop! He's **MBFG**. But I can't help it. He's **2D4**.

Luke says he hates green. The Greens beat his fav footie team.

So, I'm wearing a hot red top, but I'm a **GF** to Roz.

Why?

I put a teeny, weeny, green badge that says: I LOVE GREEN on my red top.

Kind of shows I'm not keen on her guy.

Right?

'Nice red, Abi. Top team,' says Luke when I get to hall. He smiles and my legs wobble and my heart goes bump bump.

No! Now my face is as red as my top.

Roz, **MBF**, is giving me black looks.

And Luke has blue eyes: as blue
as the sky.

'Doh! It's my last clean one,' I say,
super-fast.

What a lame lie!

Luke winks.

Roz is still giving me black looks.
I think she's going to take off like a
rocket.

Then she smiles. 'Great badge!'

'It's … uh, green,' I say. Duh to
me!

Roz snorts.

Then she gives Luke a big
smacker on his lips. Uh!

But when she gets a pack of my
fav chocs out of her bag and gives it
to me, my eyes pop.

'For me?'

'Yep!'

'For what?' I say.

'For being the best mate in the world,' she says. 'I got a B for that Art work you did with me. Thanks, Abi. You're **MBF** 4ever.'

I wish Roz hadn't said that.

I am a **RAT**.

It's true. I'm great at Art, but the pits in Maths.

Roz always helps me in Maths. She is so hot in Maths and she's mad to go to a top Uni. One day, Roz wants to go to the best and do the really hard, geeky stuff. She is sooooo clever.

Roz can count and I know she thinks three's a crowd.

But she comes up and gives me a big, happy hug. She is such a good friend and so cuddly.

I watch them both walk away and I run to the loo.

I look in the mirror to see how red my face is.

Oh no! My face is red, but it's gunky green too!

Flash back!

Brekker: I dug my face into a tub of Apple Rooty Smoothie. Apple Rooty is *very* green and icky.

Now I know why Roz was so cool. I had icky green all over my face. Thanks Roz!

Splat!

Luke thinks I luv green, when all I luv is Luke.

THREE

It's 10 p.m.

A bad day: the pits.

Mum asked me why I looked so down.

I bit her head off, so now I'm a ratty rat.

I run to my room and log on ...

Beep – msg.

Pza-Pip:

Hi, Y-me?

ILMFG too!!!!!

> It's bad. It's sad. I need 2 act
> or I'll go mad.
> _____

Oh wow!

My eyes light up. I feel great. I'm
not alone. I don't know who Pip is.
But I know she feels the same way as
me.

I'm not the only rat in town!

> _____
> **Y-me?:**
>
> OMG! Pip, thanks for your
> msg.

I don't know what 2 do. I
luv MBF too.

Pza-Pip:

Yep!

MBFG is so hot.

But MBF has been MBF for
soooo long. From way back
when we were in pre-prep.
She's ace.

Mb if I tell her, it will be OK?

Y-me?:

NOoooooooo!

No way. Mb U need a hobby?
I'm into yoga. Mum says I'm
too moody. I am so ratty
about Luke and mum's on to
me. So, OK. I'll yogi him out
of my head. Pre-prep?
What's yr school?

Pza-Pip:

Fab plan! I don't feel kind of
yogi. Hey, I'll get some

rollers and fly around the
park. Gr8! Sk8 him out of my
head. FYI – I'm at Dean Prep.
Yours?

Y-me?:

Lee Rd, School. Not a fanC
pre-prep but Gr8 fun.

Deal! We'll get fit and keep
our BFs 4ever. Even with
their 2D4 guys.

Arghgh, stop!

Pza-Pip:

LOL. Your mum's is the best plan ever.

Msg me how the yoga goes and thx for the tip.
Luv, Pza-Pip.

FOUR

Saturday.

Y-me?:

Srsly sad. At yoga got hair
stuck in zip. Str8 to 1st aid.

Now have wonky haircut.

OMG, Ruby got some px. She was swimming with her mates. Now px are on FB. CREEP!

I am zig-zag. Roz came round with chocci and some TLC. I am now a wonky rat friend.

Pza-Pip:

LOL. Pain? Me too. I sk8ed into a tree and hit my nose. Now it's bigger than my face.

I can't C my own lips.

I keep missing my food so my tee's got brekky, lunch and dins down it. Looks pretty arty! I may pin it.

Srsly? TBH. Need Plan B – 2 get Hugo out of my head.

Y-me?:

Time for plan B. ASAP.

BRB.

Pza-Pip:

OMG. Srsly sad. Erica's called in tears. Hugo told her she's getting fat. It hurt her big time.

Mb Hugo just wants her to be OK. and not fat and sad? He's so hot on keep fit. He is fit.

He's cool and wants Erica to go to fit club. WDY say?

Y-me?:

Ow! Mb he does care. But he needs to get wise. It's not what you say. It's how you say it.

He'd better be srsly 2D4 to dish that out. Can't say I know if Hugo is a totes dork or nice guy.

Pza-Pip:

Erica said he told her he luvs her and wants her to be fit

and cool. He's just a totes
good guy with a bad vocab.

Y-me?:

OK. U2U Mb Hugo's done
Erica a big fav. He's cute.
So – ta-rum! Plan B. I'm
taking up footie.

Luke's helping out at school
footie club. I luv footie. I dig
footie. Big lie.

Plan B: Find out what Hugo
likes and go for it.

Pza-Pip:

You're on. Good luck,
Beckham.

FIVE

Friday footie club and Roz is sitting staring at me.

My shorts feel too small. My tee feels too small. I feel too small.

What am I doing here? But Luke runs up.

'Hey Abi, you made it. You're in goal,' he says.

'Me? In goal? But … ' I say.

Too late!

Game on.

I'm in goal and I don't know where to look. The ball is flying all over the hall.

Bang!

No! That's a lie. The ball just hit

me on the nose then went into my net.

'Hey, that's not nice!' I cry at the kid who's in fits.

But he keeps smiling.

Five mins on and **wham!** it hits me right in the eye.

'Not funny, duh!' I say, tossing the ball out.

'Keep your eye on the ball,' says Luke, after I let in goal no. 4.

'What?'

Luke winks and I fizz.

'Sure,' I say, with two black eyes.
'I would if I could see it'.

It's **OFL**. I suck at footie.

After the game, Roz comes over
and I can see she feels sorry for me.

'Abi, you're an ace swimmer,' she
says, to try and cheer me up.

'Thanks,' I say.

But I know that I'm pants at footie
and a pants mate too.

♥

It's 8 p.m.

I log on.

Pza-Pip:

> Y-Me? Bad plan – srsly!
> Footie's OK. But Hugo loves
> boxing. So I was in our gym
> ring with Fisty Flora.

Fisty Flora looks like a fairy, but she's an Orc! She's an evil Orc!

I got 4 pins in my cheek, a fat lip and two b eyes + my fat nose. Hugo did not like my foot-work or my hits.

Well, TBH I didn't get to hit Fisty Flora in all 2 mins I was in the ring. It was a totes KO. Boy is she fast!

Y-me?:

OMG! Soooo sry.

Pza-Pip:

Hey, no probs. Just need to have a hol in A&E with my fav pizza B4 next plan.

Y-me?:

Oh no! Roz just texted. She's coming round to talk.

She knows I luv Luke. This

> is it: end of best mates.

Pza-Pip:

Bad news!

By the time Roz gets to me, I know she's been crying.

I don't like to see her so sad.

She always cheers me up when I'm low, but I can't make her feel good.

I know she hates me and is going to tell me to get lost for having the hots for her guy.

'What's up, Roz?' I ask. But I know it's no more BF 4ever.

'I've got my Maths exam back, Abi. I got top! Top!' she says.

'But, that's fab! That's ace!' I yell and jump up and down.

'No. It's not. One day, when I get to go to Uni, I won't want to. If I go to Uni, I won't see Luke,' she says,

Now I do want to jump for joy.

Not only is Roz still **MBF**, but she'll get a top place at a top Uni. She'll have to end it with Luke!

I give her a big hug.

'Hey, Roz, it's fab. You're so cool geeky. You will love Uni. You won't have to help pea-brains like me. Bet, you'll end up as one of their Profs. And anyway going is still a long way off,' I say.

But I am a big, smelly rat.

Roz smiles, but she's cut-up.

'Have you told Luke, yet?' I say.

She nods a 'no'.

Then, I feel a pang. This sucks. Roz gets top marks and she's unhappy? That is so bad.

'Hey,' I say, 'No pro. Maybe Luke will get to go too?'

But I sooooo hope that won't happen.

Time to cheer her up.

So I put on Roz's fav sci-fi movie and we just eat muffins.

♥

11 p.m.

I think Roz has gone home more chilled than when she came.

But I'm not.

I am sunk. I hate myself.

I log on.

Y-me?:

> Big prob, Pza-Pip. My mate's
> gone off Uni, for Luke.
>
> She's so geeky. She'd luv it –
> but not losing her 2D4 guy.
> Part of me thinks this is
> great! She must go to Uni.
> The other thinks I stink. I do
> LMBF. She's so kind. I'm lost.

Pza-Pip:

Hey, Y-me? You think you've got probs! Erica's cut-up.

She got A* Maths 2. But 2nite, Hugo txtd her that he's not into geeks.

He says she's a nerd and a bore. So, if she wants him to hang around, she dumps the A*s and acts like a girl. He says A*s aren't cool.

OMG! I am srsly sick. He may

be 2D4 – but what? He got a C in Maths. She is gutted.

Y-me?:

No way! Hugo is an MCP. He needs to hit the pigsty.

Act like a girl? What's that? The pits.

Erica needs to dump him, ZOMG.

Pza-Pip:

Let's meet F2F. School footie
this Sat – Dean Prep v. Lee Rd
at the rec.

Y-me?:

Plan! Luke's playing! I'll be
in my red tee!

Pza-Pip:

I'll be Green Queen.

SIX

It's Saturday and I'm waiting for Pza-Pip.

I wonder what she looks like. I can't wait to see her and talk like mad.

I'm so sad for Erica. I mean, who'd want to be with a goon like Hugo?

I look and look, but I can't see Pza-Pip, the Green Queen.

Dean Prep team are in blue and my school and Luke are in red.

NTS if Blues beat Reds, do not wear blue tees.

I'm so peeved that Pza-Pip's not here.

But then Roz rocks up and guess what? Roz is a Green Queen.

I gulp.

'Hi, Y-me?,' says Roz.

My mouth falls open.

'Pza-Pip?' I cry.

I put my hands to my face. I want to run away. I am the rat.

'You really are Pza-Pip?' I cry again.

'Yes, I'm Erica too,' says Roz sadly. 'I needed to talk about you, me and ... '

She looks across at Luke.

My mouth is still wide open. Duh to me!

'How did you know it was me?' I say.

'I didn't – not at first. Then it hit me,' said Roz.

'But, Roz,' I say, 'Then – Hugo's not for real?'

'Oh Hugo is for real,' says Roz. 'Hugo is Luke. It was all about Luke. It was Luke who called me fat and told me not to be such a geek and Luke who said, "Drop the Maths and act like a fun girl." So, I'm a fat, un-fun girl.'

She's about to cry and I feel so bad for her.

I look across at Luke as he kicks about and **BANG!** all I see is one big, fat ego.

This is for real. Luke is Hugo.

I am sunk.

'Abi! It's OK,' says Roz, trying to smile. 'Luke's dumped me. I'm cool if you want to hook up with him. I'll still be BF 4ever.'

My head is in a spin.

She hugs me and now I want to cry.

SEVEN

> **Y-me?:**
>
> Hey, Pza-Pip. On Sat, Hugo
> txtd and asked me out. Joke!
> It felt soooo good to tell him
> to go jump! Creep!

He srsly thinks I'd like him when he's hurt MBF. I told him, I'm into guys who rate girls for what they are: fat, skinny, geeks and all .

I luv MBF. She's tops. Thnx for the hugs on Sat. I have missed you sooooo much.

BTW, pleeeeeze help with my Maths for Monday?

Pza-Pip:

WOW! Luv U, Y-me? I've

missed you, big time.

Brill! Maths and hot choc on Sun. T.I.M.E. xxxx

Y-me?:

Hey, I'm so happy.

Pizza 2?

ILMBF 2– 4ever!

MORE GREAT READS IN THE PROMISES SERIES

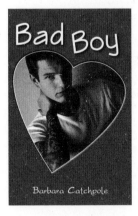

Bad Boy

by Barbara Catchpole

Taylor has had some disastrous boyfriends. There was the smelly computer geek who wrote code all day, and there was the one who was football mad and only wore Liverpool shirts.

Then Taylor meets Josh. He is tall, hunky and drop-dead gorgeous. It's perfect! Or is it?

ch@t

by Barbara Catchpole

'Are you out of your tiny looney-tunes mind?'

That's what Gina's sister says when she finds out Gina is chatting online with a boy she doesn't know.

But Gina loves talking to Chatboy1 – he makes her laugh and he *understands* her. But what will happen when Gina tries to meet him IRL?

MORE GREAT READS
IN THE PROMISES SERIES

Picture Him

by Jo Cotterill

Aliya loves taking photos. She talks with a stammer, but who needs words when you have pictures?

But when Aliya looks at her latest series of photos ('zombie princess', taken with her friend Zoe) she sees a murky figure in the background of many of them. Is she being stalked?

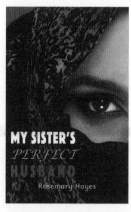

My Sister's Perfect Husband

by Rosemary Hayes

Laila's older sister Mina is eighteen, and her Pashtun family feel it's time they found her a husband.

They introduce her to several suitable young men, but Mina scowls at each one, putting them off as much as she can.

So Laila sets about finding the perfect husband for her sister.